Folk Tales
for Reading and Telling

Leila Berg, writer, editor, journalist, critic, has run a
nursery school in her own house at the same time as
forty or so boys and girls were holding meetings and
folk-song sessions in her cellar. Her friends are of all
ages from babies onward, and she says she learns an
enormous amount from them. Her husband is an
engineer, her daughter is an actress, her son is an art
student. She believes firmly in equality – that is, she
says, 'the equal right of everyone to be different'.

D1464766

Also by Leila Berg in Piccolo

The Little Car has a Day Out

Leila Berg

Folk tales

for reading and telling

illustrated by George Him

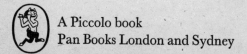

A Piccolo book
Pan Books London and Sydney

First published 1966 by Brockhampton Press Ltd
This edition published 1976 by Pan Books Ltd,
Cavaye Place, London SW10 9PG
4th printing 1977
Text © Leila Berg 1966
New illustrations © George Him 1976
ISBN 0 330 24380 2
Printed and bound in Great Britain by
Richard Clay (The Chaucer Press) Ltd, Bungay, Suffolk

Contents

with country of origin and approximate duration

This book is intended to be read to young children, and to be read by children as soon as they have mastered the art of reading on their own. But, above all, stories, especially the traditional folk tales, are for telling, and the Author's Note at the end of this book is addressed to those adults who would like to be story-tellers

Mr Wolf and his tail

Now this is the tale of a wolf,
who would have done better
to keep his mouth shut.
And this is the way I tell it

One day Mr Wolf was out walking when some big dogs began to chase him. They chased and they chased, and they nearly caught him. But luckily Mr Wolf suddenly saw a cave in the mountain. It was just big enough for him to get inside, and he dashed in quickly. The cave was too small for the big dogs to get in, so they had to stay outside.

Mr Wolf panted and panted, 'Huh-huh-huh,'

till he got his breath back. Then when he felt
better, he thought he had been very clever to get
into this cave. So he began to talk out loud. 'Feet,
feet,' he said. 'What did *you* do to help me to get
into this cave?'

'Why, we jumped over the rocks and the rivers,
and we brought you here,' said his four feet.

'So you did,' said the wolf. '*Good* feet!'

'And what did *you* do?' he said to his two ears.
'What did *you* do, ears, to help me?'

'Why, we listened to the right, and we listened
to the left,' said his two ears. 'We heard where the
dogs were coming, so we could tell you which was
the right way to go.'

'So you did,' said the wolf. '*Good* ears!

'And what did *you* do?' said Mr Wolf to his two
eyes. 'What did *you* do to help me?'

'Why, we looked,' said his two eyes. 'We pointed
out the right way. We found this cave.'

'So you did,' said Mr Wolf. '*Good* eyes.'

Then Mr Wolf said, 'What a fine fellow I am to
have such good feet, such good ears, and such good
eyes. I *am* clever.' And he leaned over to pat
himself on the back. When he did this, he saw his
tail. 'Oh,' said Mr Wolf. 'Oho! And what did *you*
do, tail? I bet you did nothing at all. You just hung
there on the end of me, expecting me to carry you
along, and you did nothing at all to help. Why, I
bet you nearly let the dogs get hold of me. What
did you do?'

The tail was so cross at being spoken to like this, that he said, 'I'll tell you what I did. I waved to the dogs to tell them to come on and catch you!'

'You *bad* tail!' shouted Mr Wolf. 'You bad, bad tail!' And he turned around and bit it as hard as he could. Then he shouted very angrily, 'Get out of here at once! You bad old tail! Get out of this cave!'

And he pushed his tail out of the cave. But when he pushed his tail out, of course, he went out with it. And the big dogs were waiting outside, listening to every silly word, and they caught him.

Rabbit and Elephant

Now this is a tale of a lazy, greedy elephant.
And this is the way I tell it

Rabbit and Elephant were friends. One day
they were very hungry. 'We'll have to do some
work,' said Rabbit. 'Then we can get some food.'

They went together to a farmer who lived
nearby, and Rabbit said, 'Will you give us some
beans to eat if we work in your fields?'

'Certainly I will,' said the farmer. 'But you'll
have to work properly, you know.'

'Of course we will,' said Rabbit. Elephant said
nothing. When the farmer looked at him, he just
made a sort of coughing noise.

Now the farmer could see Rabbit and Elephant
were really hungry, so he gave them the beans
right away, and they put them in the pot to cook
while they were working. So there were the beans
cooking away in the pot, and there were Rabbit
and Elephant working in the fields.

Rabbit worked and worked. But Elephant
didn't work at all. He kept saying how hot it was,
and how hard it was, and that his foot hurt, and

that his ear hurt, and that the grass was prickly, and that something was biting him. And he'd keep going away to have a drink, and whenever he came back he'd say, 'Oh look, you've hardly anything left to do. And look how much I have!' So Rabbit thought, 'Oh dear, I suppose I'll have to help him, or he'll never get finished.'

And that's how it happened that when Rabbit had finished all her own work, instead of sitting down and eating her beans – for she was very hungry – she started on Elephant's work instead. Even then, Elephant didn't help. He said he had to go off to get some banana leaves to keep his forehead cool, because he had a headache.

Rabbit worked away, hungrier and hotter, till it was all done. Then Elephant came back, and the two of them walked over to their cooking-pot, and looked at their beans cooking away there. Oh they did smell good.

Rabbit was just going to take some at last, when Elephant said, 'Don't take them yet. I just have to have a wash. You won't start without me, will you?' So Rabbit, who was so very hungry after all the work she'd done, looked sadly at the bubbling, steaming beans, and said politely, 'No, of course I won't start without you, Elephant.'

Off went Elephant to the river, and hid in the tall, wavy grass. And there he quickly undid his sixteen buttons – for in those days an Elephant's coat still buttoned down the front with sixteen

buttons – and he stepped out of his coat, one leg, two legs, three legs, four legs, folded it tidily and left it on the grass.

Well, Rabbit was sitting by the beans, wishing Elephant would hurry up, when suddenly –

'RRRRRah!' something frightful rushed at her, something enormous. It was as big as an elephant, but so peculiar-looking. Rabbit left the beans, and ran and ran.

It was a little while before she felt brave enough to come back. She came through the grass, stepping very quietly on the tips of her toes. It was all right. The monster had gone. But so had the beans.

Soon Elephant came back from the river. He looked very happy. 'Are the beans ready?' he called.

'Oh, Elephant,' said Rabbit. 'A terrible thing has happened. A monster has come and eaten all the beans.'

'I don't believe it,' said Elephant. 'You've eaten them yourself, you greedy thing.'

'Oh no,' said Rabbit. 'You know I wouldn't.'

'Well, it can't be helped,' said Elephant. 'We'll just have to go to bed without any beans.'

So that was how the first day ended.

Next day the farmer gave them more work and more beans. They put them on to cook the same as before, and Rabbit worked hard, so hard, while Elephant did nothing. He said his toe was blistered, and his tail had got bent, and he had something in his eye.

And at last Elephant went away to wash, and in the long, wavy grass he undid all his sixteen buttons and stepped out of his coat, one leg, two legs, three legs, four legs, folded it tidily and left it on the grass. And you know what happened next. Rabbit, sitting by the bubbling beans, was chased away by an enormous monster, as big as an elephant, but so peculiar-looking. And when she came back, stepping so quietly on the tips of her toes, the monster had gone – and so had the beans.

'I bet you ate them yourself,' said Elephant, when Rabbit told him.

'No, I didn't,' said Rabbit. 'You know I didn't.'

'Well, it can't be helped,' said Elephant. 'We'll have to go to bed without any beans.'

'All right,' said Rabbit. 'But you know what I'm going to do? Before I go to bed, I'm going to look for some wood, and I'm going to make a bow and arrow, and if that monster comes again to take our beans, I'll shoot him dead.'

Later that evening, Elephant said to Rabbit, 'Oh, Rabbit, did you make a bow and arrow?'

'Yes, I did,' said Rabbit.

'You'd better let me have a look at it,' said Elephant. 'I know a lot about bows and arrows, and I can tell you if it's a good one.'

So Rabbit brought her bow and arrow, and Elephant looked at it and said, 'Mmmmmm. Not bad at all. There's just a little bit here, I'll make right for you.' And he got out his knife and cut away for a bit, and at last he said, 'Ah, that's better. That'll be all right now. I'm glad you showed me that.'

Then they went to bed and that was how the second day ended.

Next day, they went to work again, while the beans cooked in the pot. Rabbit worked hard. Elephant made excuses. Then just the same as before, the monster came rushing at Rabbit as she sat by the cooking-pot waiting for Elephant to come back from the river. But this time Rabbit picked up her bow and arrow and shot at him. 'Crack!' The bow broke. Wasn't that just the place where Elephant had been cutting it with his knife?

Well, off ran Rabbit as fast as she could, with the monster after her. When she came back, all the beans were gone.

'Did you catch the monster?' called Elephant.

'No. The bow broke.'

'Really! I am surprised!' And Elephant hid his smile with his curly trunk.

Rabbit didn't notice Elephant smiling, but she had suddenly begun to wonder what an Elephant would look like if he undid all the sixteen buttons of his coat and stepped right out of it, one leg, two legs, three legs, four legs. She wondered about this all evening, for by now she was very hungry indeed. The next morning she got up very early and made herself a new bow and arrow and hid them in the grass.

Everything happened the same as before. Rabbit worked hard. Elephant did nothing. He was tired, he felt sick, he was thirsty. Off he went to the river at last, to have his wash. And in a minute or two, on came the roaring monster.

But this time as soon as Rabbit saw the roaring monster, she picked up her new bow and arrow from the grass, and aimed very carefully.

'Ow!' shouted Elephant. 'You horrid thing! You've hurt me! What did you do that for? Fancy being so mean, just for a few beans! I'll probably die!'

But Rabbit was very angry. 'A fine friend you are!' she said. 'You won't die. It's only a prick. Now go and wash yourself properly this time, and put on your coat, and don't you dare play any tricks on me again!'

So Elephant went slowly back to the river, and really *did* wash himself this time, and put on his coat, and did up all the sixteen buttons, and behaved properly. And Rabbit sat down by the bubbling, steaming beans, and, at last, ate them all up.

The big white pussy-cat

Now this tale happened at Christmas-time.
And this is the way I tell it

Once upon a time there was a man. And one
day he caught a bear. It was a very fine bear, so he
thought he would give it to the King.

So off they went, the man and the bear, tramp,
tramp, tramp, to see the King. They hadn't gone
very far when they came to a little house. And
because it was very dark and they were afraid it
was going to snow – because it was winter-time and
so cold – they were pleased to see the little house.
They knocked at the door to ask if they could come
in. They thought, you see, that perhaps they could
sleep inside in a cosy bed, instead of outside in the
snow. For it would be a long time yet before they
got to the King.

A man answered the door. 'May we come and
sleep in your house?' said the bear-man.

'Oh dear, no,' said the man who opened the
door. His name was Halvor.

'But it's cold out here,' said the bear-man.

'I know,' said Halvor.

'So may we come in?' said the bear-man.

'Oh dear, no,' said Halvor.

'But it's dark, and it's starting to snow,' said the bear-man.

'I know,' said Halvor.

'So may we come in?'

'Oh dear, no.'

'Well,' said the bear-man, 'that's a funny way to talk. Don't you want to help us and be kind to us?'

'Oh, I would very much like to help you,' said Halvor. 'But you see, it's Christmas-time. And every Christmas-time an enormous crowd of trolls come tearing into our house. They bang about, and they break the dishes, and they throw things, and they scream and shout, and they chase us right out of the house! Every Christmas-time! Isn't it a shame for our poor children – they never have a proper Christmas because of those trolls!'

'Oh, is it just trolls that are bothering you?' said the bear-man. 'We don't care about trolls. Just let us in and we'll sleep on the floor.'

So in the end Halvor let the man and the bear come in. And the bear lay down, while the man sat by the fire. And Halvor and his wife and their three children started to get the Christmas dinner ready; but, do you know, they did it with such sad faces because they knew that the trolls were going to chase them out before they could eat any of it.

Well, the next day was Christmas Day and they put that lovely dinner on the table. And sure enough, down the chimney came the trolls! Through the window came the trolls! Out of the fireplace came the trolls! And they banged about, and they broke the dishes, and they threw things, and they screamed and shouted. Halvor and his wife and the three children got up and ran out of the kitchen and out of the house and into the shed in the garden, and they locked the door.

But the man and the bear just sat still and watched. My, oh my, those trolls were naughty.

They put their feet on the table, and they put their
tails on the table, and they threw milk about, and
they squashed up the cakes with their dirty toes,
and they licked the jelly with their long, long
tongues. The littlest ones were the worst of all.
They climbed up the curtains, and they got on
the shelves, and they started to throw down all

the jars of jam and jars of honey and jars of
pickled onions, right off the shelves. Smash!
Crash! Oh, there was a mess!

Well, at last one of the littlest, naughtiest trolls
suddenly saw the bear lying there very quiet and
good. And the little troll found a piece of sausage
and stuck it on a fork, and waved it about under
the bear's nose, and shouted, 'Pussy, pussy! Have
a sausage!' Oh, he was wild, that little troll! He

poked the bear's nose with the fork. And just when the bear snapped at the sausage, he pulled it away so that the bear couldn't get it.

Then the great white bear was very, very angry. He got up from the floor, and he opened his mouth wide, and he roared at the top of his voice like

thunder, and he chased those trolls right out of the house, big ones and little ones, those with tails and those without.

'Good boy!' said the bear-man. '*Good* boy!' And he gave him a whole sausage to eat. And he ate it nicely, making hardly any mess at all.

Then the bear-man called out, 'You can come out, Halvor, you and your wife and your three little children. The trolls have gone away. My bear chased them out.' So Halvor and his wife and his three children unlocked the wood-shed and came out and came back to the house. They swept up the mess, and they scrubbed the table, and they picked up all the broken bits and put them in the dustbin. Then they all sat down to eat everything the trolls had left – and luckily they had left quite a lot, and it was very nice indeed. Then they all went to bed.

Next day, the bear-man said to Halvor, 'Thank you for having us. Now we must go to see the King.' And away went the man and the bear, and Halvor never saw them again, so I expect they found the King.

Now when Christmas Eve came round again the next year, Halvor was out chopping wood in the forest. Suddenly he heard someone calling far away through the trees. 'Halvor! Halvor!'

'What is it?' shouted Halvor.

'Have you still got your big white pussy-cat with you?'

'Yes, I have!' shouted Halvor. 'She's lying in front of the fire at home this minute. And she's got seven kittens now, and each of them is bigger and fiercer than she is herself. Now! What do you say to that?'

'Then, we'll never, never come to see you again!' shouted all the trolls.

And do you know, they never did, never. And now Halvor and his wife and his three children can always eat up their Chrismas dinner just the same as everyone else.

The greedy spider

*Now this is the tale of a spider
who could never miss a party.
And this is the way I tell it*

Once there was a spider who liked going to parties,
even when he was not invited.

One day he saw some ants running about on the
ground, telling each other the news. He could see
it was exciting news from the way they were
running. He was sure they were telling each other
about a party.

He let himself down on his spider's rope, so that
he could hear where the party was. But just as he
was near them ... 'What'll I do, what'll I do?'
mumbled a silly wood-pigeon up in a tree; and he
couldn't hear a word.

He tried again. He let the wind blow him a little
closer, and he listened very hard. But ... 'What'll
I do, what'll I do?' cried the silly wood-pigeon up
in the tree; and he didn't hear a word.

'I *will* go to the party,' said the spider. 'I'll send
for my four children. They'll know where it is.'

So he sent for his four children, and they came
swinging along in the wind at the end of their four
ropes.

27

The first one said, 'Rabbit is having a party. But he doesn't know what day.'

'Well, tie a rope round my middle,' said the spider. 'Then when the party starts, you can pull on the rope and I'll come along.'

So the spider's first child tied a rope round the spider's middle, and then blew away in the wind.

Then the second child came swinging along on the wind. He said, 'Oh, Antelope is having a party. But he doesn't know when it will be.'

'Then, tie a rope round my middle,' said the spider, 'and when the party starts, you can pull on the rope and I'll come along.'

So the spider's second child tied a rope round the spider's middle, and then swung away in the wind.

The spider's third child came, and he said Leopard was having a party. And the spider's fourth child came, and he said Frog was having a party. But neither of them knew what day. So each of them tied a rope round spider's middle, and swung away on the wind.

One beautiful evening when the moon was full, all the four ropes round Spider's middle began to pull at once. One pulled him eastwards. One pulled him westwards. One pulled him this way. One pulled him that way.

'Stop!' cried Spider. 'I'll be cut in half.' But none of his four children could hear him.

Spider felt very ill, *very* ill. Just when he

thought he really *would* be cut in half, the ropes snapped. So Spider didn't get to any of the parties, and ever since, his middle has been as tiny as can be. But do you think it has stopped him wanting to go to parties where he isn't invited? No, it has not! In fact, if you look, you'll sometimes see him swinging in the wind on his long rope, trying to hear what the ants are saying.

Mr Fox

Now this is the tale of a fox
and all the things that went into his bag.
And this is the way I tell it

One day Mr Fox was digging by his tree when he found a big fat bumble-bee. So he put it in his bag.

Then he walked, and he walked, and he walked, till he came to a house. And in the house there was a little black woman sweeping the floor.

'Good morning,' said Mr Fox.

'Good morning,' said the little black woman.

'May I leave my bag here? I want to go to Squantum's house.'

'Yes, certainly.'

'Very well then,' said Mr Fox. 'But mind you don't look in my bag.'

'Oh, I won't,' said the little black woman.

So off went Mr Fox, trot, trot, trot-trot-trot, to Squantum's house.

As soon as he was gone, I'm afraid the little black woman *did* look in the bag. She just peeped in. And out flew the big fat bumble-bee! And the little black woman's cock-a-doodle-doo ran and gobbled him up.

Presently back came Mr Fox. He looked at his bag and he said, 'Where is my big fat bumble-bee?'

And the little black woman said, 'I'm dreadfully sorry, but I'm afraid I did look in your bag, and the big fat bumble-bee flew out, and my cock-a-doodle-doo gobbled him up.'

'Oh really!' said Mr Fox. 'Then I shall take your cock-a-doodle-doo instead.'

And he took the little black woman's cock-a-doodle-doo and put that in the bag instead. Then off he went.

He walked, and he walked, and he walked, until he came to a house. And in this house there was a little red woman darning socks.

'Good morning,' said Mr Fox.

'Oh, good morning,' said the little red woman.

'May I leave my bag here while I go to Squintum's house?'

'Yes, certainly,' said the little red woman.

'Very well then,' said Mr Fox. 'But mind you don't look in my bag.'

'I won't,' said the little red woman.

So off went Mr Fox, trot, trot, trot-trot-trot, to Squintum's house.

As soon as he was gone, I'm afraid the little red woman *did* look in the bag. She just peeped in, and out flew the cock-a-doodle-doo. And the little red woman's pig chased him down the lane.

Presently back came Mr Fox. He looked at his bag, and he said, 'Oho! Where is my cock-a-doodle-doo?'

And the little red woman said, 'I'm very sorry, but I did open your bag. And your cock-a-doodle-doo flew out, and my pig chased him down the lane.'

'Very well,' said Mr Fox. 'I shall take your pig instead.' And he put the little red woman's pig in the bag.

Then off he went. He walked, and he walked, and he walked, till he came to a house. And in this house there was a little yellow woman washing the dishes.

'Good morning,' said Mr Fox.

'Oh, good morning,' said the little yellow woman.

'May I leave my bag here while I go to Squeeeentum's house?'

'Yes, certainly.'

'Very well then. But mind you don't look in my bag.'

'No, I won't,' said the little yellow woman.

Then off went Mr Fox, trot, trot, trot-trot-trot, to Squeeeentum's house.

As soon as he was gone, the little yellow woman *did* look in the bag. She just peeped in, and out jumped the pig. And the little yellow woman's little boy took a stick and chased him right out of the house.

Pretty soon, back came Mr Fox. He looked at his bag and he said, 'Dear me. Where is my pig?'

And the little yellow woman said, 'I'm frightfully sorry, but I'm afraid I did look in your bag. And the pig jumped out, and my little boy took a stick and chased him right out of the house.'

'My goodness,' said Mr Fox. 'Then I shall have to take your little boy instead.' And he took the little yellow woman's little boy, and put him in the bag.

Then he walked, and he walked, and he walked, until he came to a house. And in this house there was a little green woman making gingerbread. At one side of her sat four little girls. And on the other side sat a big black dog.

'Good morning,' said Mr Fox.

'Good morning,' said the little green woman.

'May I leave my bag here while I go to Squoooontum's house?'

'Yes, certainly.'

'Very well then. But mind you don't look in my bag.' Then off went Mr Fox, trot, trot, trot-trot-trot, to Squoooontum's house.

Now as soon as he was gone, the lovely smell of the gingerbread came out of the oven, and it smelled so good, so good that all the four little girls called out, 'Oh, Mummy, Mummy, may we have some gingerbread?' And the little boy in the bag called out, 'Oh, Auntie, Auntie, may I have some gingerbread?'

Well, of course, as soon as the little green woman heard a little boy calling out of the bag, she undid the bag at once. And out jumped the little boy. And so that Mr Fox wouldn't notice anything, the little green woman put the big black dog in the bag instead.

Presently, back came Mr Fox. He looked at the bag, and it still looked all bumpy and knobbly. So he thought it was just the same as before. He picked it up and off he went.

He walked, and he walked, and he walked, till he came to a good place to sit down. Then he sat down. And he untied the bag. And out jumped the big black dog. He was so hungry because he hadn't had any gingerbread yet, that he gobbled up Mr Fox completely.

And back in the little house, the little green

woman took the gingerbread out of the oven. And the four little girls and the one little boy sat down at the table and they ate it all up. Except for one piece that they saved for their mummy because she baked it, and one piece that they gave to the dog when he came home, for eating up Mr Fox.

The Billy-Goats Gruff

Now this is the tale of three goats.
And this is the way I tell it

Once upon a time there were three billy-goats
Gruff. They were all called Gruff. That was their
name.

At the end of their field was a hill, and the
billy-goats Gruff liked to go up the hillside to eat
the juicy green grass and make themselves fat. But
to get to the hill they had to cross a bridge that
went over a little river; and under the bridge lived
a troll, with eyes as big as saucers and a nose as long
as a poker.

Now one day the three billy-goats Gruff decided
to go up the hillside to make themselves fat. First
came the youngest billy-goat Gruff, trip-trap, on to
the bridge.

'Who's that running on to my bridge?' roared
the troll.

'It's only me, the littlest billy-goat Gruff. I'm
just going on to the hillside to make myself fat.'

'Don't you dare to come on to my bridge, or I'll
gobble you up!'

'Oh, don't gobble me up. I'm much too little.
Eat my big brother. He's just coming now.'

'Oh, all right,' said the troll.

So the youngest billy-goat Gruff ran, trip-trap, right over the bridge and on to the hillside.

Presently along came the second billy-goat Gruff, trip-trap-trip, on to the bridge.

'Who's that running on to my bridge?' roared the troll.

'Oh, it's only me, the second billy-goat Gruff. I'm just going up the hillside to make myself fat.'

'Don't you dare come on to my bridge, or I'll gobble you up!'

'Oh, don't gobble me up. I'm much too little. Eat my big brother instead. He's just coming now.'

'Oh, all right,' said the troll.

So the second billy-goat Gruff ran, trip-trap-trip, right over the bridge and on to the hillside.

Presently along came the biggest billy-goat Gruff, trip-trap-trip-trap, on to the bridge.

'Who's that running on to my bridge?' roared the troll.

'It's me, the biggest billy-goat Gruff. I'm going up the hillside to make myself fat.'

'Don't you dare come on to my bridge,' roared the troll, 'or I'll gobble you up!'

'Gobble me up!' said the biggest billy-goat Gruff. 'Gobble me up! Oh no you won't!' And he ran at the troll with his long horns, and he tossed him up in the air, and he tossed him down in the water. Then he went over the bridge, trip-trap, trip-trap, and on to the hillside to join his brothers. And all the three billy-goats Gruff ate the juicy green grass, till they were so fat they could scarcely get home again.

The little man with big feet

*Now this is a tale of a front door
that had to be put at the back.
And this is the way I tell it*

There was once a good old farmer, and he lived
with his wife in a little white, tidy white, cottage.
Every night, just before they went to bed, his wife
did the washing up and the old farmer did the
drying. And then, while his wife swept the kitchen,
the old farmer would see to the bucket of
washing-up water.

There was only one place to empty the
washing-up water. And that was outside the door,
over a little low wall. Full of all sorts of things that
washing-up water would be – tea-leaves and
potato peelings, apple peel and onion skins, and
egg-shells too as likely as not. And of course it was
very dirty, for it was the washing-up water for the
whole day.

Now one night, the old man picked up the
bucket as usual. Outside the door he went, and
tossed the water over the wall.

'Oh dear, I wish you wouldn't do that!' said someone.

The old man turned round. There was a funny little chap. He was very small, except for his feet, and they were enormous.

'But I always do this,' said the farmer. 'I've been doing it for thirty years!'

'I know you have,' said the little man. 'Thirty years! Imagine that! Thirty years of washing-up water! Oh dear!' he said. And again, 'Oh dear!'

'But what's the matter?' said the old farmer. 'It's only our washing-up water.'

'Oh dear,' said the little man again. 'There's only one thing to do. You'll have to get on my foot.'

'Get on your foot!' said the old farmer. 'What ever for?'

'Then you'll know,' said the little man.

So the farmer got on to the little man's foot. He had very big feet, as I've told you. The farmer looked over the wall where he always swished the washing-up water. And instead of just the grass and the stones that he generally saw, he saw right down through a kind of crack in the earth, a little street just like his own street, and in the street a little white cottage just like his own little white cottage.

But what a dreadful state that little white cottage was in. Potato peelings all over the chimney, tea-leaves splashed on the windows,

onion skins and apple peel all over the roof, and greasy, dirty water dripping down the walls. 'Now you see what you've been doing,' said the little man in a sad voice.

'I'd no idea!' said the old farmer. 'I'd no idea!'

'You've been doing it for thirty years,' said the little man. 'Can you imagine what a job we have to keep it clean? Why, sometimes the water goes down the chimney and puts the fire out. And imagine what it's like when there's washing on the line! It makes my wife cry!'

The old farmer was very upset, because he had no idea there was a little street down there in a crack in the ground where he poured the washing-up water.

'Well, I don't know what to do,' he said. 'I have to pour it somewhere. But we can't have that mess all over your house. No, certainly we can't have that, not with your wife crying and all.'

'Well, get off my foot now,' said the little man, 'and let's have a little think about it.' So the old man got off the little man's foot, and now he couldn't see the street or the house any more, just the grass and the stones that he'd always seen, and the little man.

They sat down together on the little low wall, and they didn't say a word. They just thought and thought. But all they could think was 'Oh dear!' and that wasn't much use. So at last the little man said, 'I'll come back in three days, and perhaps you'll have thought of something then. You will try, won't you?'

'Oh, I will try, I really will, I promise you,' said the old farmer. And he went into the cottage with the bucket.

As soon as he was in the kitchen he told his wife about it, and she was just as upset as he was. But what could they do? They had to pour the water somewhere.

The next night, the old farmer went slowly out of the front door and poured the water over the wall. What else could he do? And the next night the old farmer went sadly out of the front door and poured the water over the wall. What else could he do? The next day the farmer's wife had an idea. At last. And when the old farmer went out of the front door that evening, he knew what to do.

The little man with big feet was waiting for him by the wall. 'I certainly do hope you've thought of something,' he said. 'My wife has been crying all day.'

'Yes, we *have* thought of something,' said the old farmer. 'We have. Do you know what we're going to do? We're going to make a different door round the other side of the house. Then the washing-up water won't bother you at all.'

'Would you go to all that trouble?' said the little man. 'You'd have to get the builders in, you know.'

'Well, we must,' said the old farmer. 'It'll be

an expense, I know. But we can't keep making that mess all over your house.'

So he called in the builders the very next day, and the builders bricked up the old door so that it wasn't there any more, and made a new front door at the back.

And after that, the farmer and his wife would often find a silver coin pushed under the new door on a Saturday night. So they were never sorry they had called the builders in, and had the front door put at the back.

The little blue caps

*Now this is the tale of a
fisherman who sailed through the air
instead of the water.
And this is the way I tell it*

Once upon a time there was a fisherman. His
name was Ian. Every day he used to go out fishing
in his boat. But one day the sea was so rough and so
wild that he couldn't go fishing. So he decided he
would mend his boat instead.

He began looking about on the hill for a good,
strong piece of wood, just the size he needed to
mend his boat. He was looking and looking and not
finding it at all, when a mist came up and the day
began to grow dark. 'Oh, I'd better give up looking
for the wood, and get back home,' he said to
himself. 'If I stay on the hillside till the mist gets
thick, I shan't be able to see where I am, and I'll
get lost and never see my little house again.'

So he stopped looking for the wood to mend his
boat, and started off home. But the mist was
already thick, and he did get lost.

Suddenly through the clouds of mist he came
right up to a house. He knew there was someone in

because there was a light in the window. He banged on the door. Thump! 'Please let me in,' he called. 'I'm lost in the mist.' But no one came. He banged again. Thump! 'Please let me in. I'm lost in the mist.' But still no one came. So he banged louder than ever, banged and banged till his hand hurt. Thump! Thump! Thump! 'Please, please let me in. I'm lost in the mist.'

And then, at last, the door opened a teeny crack. And there was a little old woman, peeping at him with her eyes screwed up. 'What do you want?' she said crossly.

'I want to come in,' said Ian. 'It's thick with mist, and dark out here, and I'm lost, so please will you let me come in to stay till morning, when I can see my way home again?'

The old woman peeped at him and sniffed and grumbled. But at last she said, 'All right. You can come in.'

So in he came, right into the kitchen. There was a big, warm fire burning, and that was good, and at each side of the fire sat another little woman – three little old women in the house together. And they never said a word to Ian, not any of them, not one word. So he didn't say a word either. He lay down on the floor by the side of the fire and pretended to go to sleep. But he didn't really go to sleep. He watched the little old women.

Now the little old women thought he really was asleep. So they went to a big box in the corner of the room and they lifted the lid. Then one of them took out a blue woolly cap, and she put it on her head, and she said, 'Carlisle!' And do you know, she vanished away! She'd gone! She wasn't there any more.

Then the second little woman took a blue woolly cap out of the box and put it on, and she

said, 'Carlisle!' And *she* vanished. She wasn't there any more.

And then the third little woman took a blue woolly cap out of the chest, and popped it on her head and said, 'Carlisle!' and *she* vanished. *She* wasn't there any more.

'What an extraordinary thing,' said Ian. 'First there were three little old women here, and now there are none at all. Only me. I wonder if there are any more blue woolly caps in that chest?' So he had a look. There was. Just one more.

He took it out, and he popped it on his head and said, 'Carlisle!' – just like the little old women. And *he* vanished. He went flying and swirling and crossing and curling away and away and away, to goodness knows where. Then suddenly down he crashed, with a bump and a thump and a clackety clump. Where was he? Down in a cellar with the three old women.

And all around them were bottles of different kinds and different shapes and different sizes. And the three little old women were tasting all the bottles and having a party.

But when they saw Ian come down with a bump and a thump and a clackety clump in the middle of them, they settled their blue woolly caps on their heads and fast as fast shouted 'Kintail, back again!' And they were gone, first one, then two, then three.

'What an extraordinary thing,' said Ian. 'First there were three old women. And now there are none. Only me.'

Well, this time Ian didn't want to follow them. He was quite happy where he was. He tasted all the bottles, and he sipped them and licked them and drank them, till at last he had drunk so much and got so sticky that he fell fast asleep.

Now would you believe it, the place where Ian was lying fast asleep among all this shocking muddle was the Bishop of Carlisle's wine cellar.

You remember the three old women had shouted,
'Carlisle!' when they had popped on their little
blue caps. Well, there you are!

Naturally, when the Bishop of Carlisle's
servants came down the next morning and saw all
the mess – all the broken bottles, and the corks
out, and the stickiness, and the pools and the

puddles and the muddle – they were very angry indeed. 'You bad, *bad* man!' they shouted at Ian, and they took him off to the Bishop.

'Take off your little blue cap,' they shouted at him. 'It's very rude to keep on your cap when you talk to the Bishop.' And they snatched it off. Then they tied him to a big piece of wood.

Ian was very frightened. He didn't know what

the Bishop would do to him for breaking into his wine cellar in the middle of the night and making such a mess there.

So what did he do? He said, 'Please, sir, may I have my cap back?' And the second the Bishop gave it him back, he popped it on his head and shouted, 'Kintail, back again,' just like the three old women had done. And he vanished. Which was a very good thing, for goodness knows what the Bishop would have done to him.

He went flying and swirling and crossing and curling away and away and away, to goodness knows where. Then down he came with a bump and a thump and a clackety clump. There he was back on his own hill in the bright morning. Only I'm afraid he was tied to a big piece of wood.

Well, luckily he saw an old man coming up the hill, so he called out, 'Please, old man, will you untie me from this piece of wood?' And the old man said, 'Of course,' and untied him right away – at least, as soon as he could get up to him, because old people go rather slowly up hills, and his old fingers were rather stiff for untying knots.

Ian said, 'Thank you,' of course. And then the old man said, 'What ever did you want with that piece of wood?' And Ian remembered what he wanted with it. He remembered that right at the very beginning of this story, he'd been looking for a piece of wood to mend his boat. And now he had it. It was just the right size.

'That's for mending my boat,' he told the old man. 'The Bishop of Carlisle gave it to me.'

'Fancy that!' said the old man. Then they both said, 'Goodbye,' and they each went home.

Little Dog Turpie

Now this is the tale of a very good dog.
And this is the way I tell it

Once upon a time there was a little old man and
a little old woman, and they lived together in a
little old house with their Little Dog Turpie.

Now out in the woods lived the Hobyahs. Every
night they came running towards the house, up,
up, on their long toes, creeping, creeping, through
the soft grass, waving their wild tails, came the
Hobyahs. And they shouted, 'Break down the
house, carry off the little old man, eat up the little
old woman!' But Little Dog Turpie always heard
them coming, and he would bark and bark and
bark, 'Wow, wow!' till they all ran away.

The little old man and the little old woman
didn't know about the Hobyahs, because Little
Dog Turpie always frightened them away. But one
night the old man sat up in bed and said, 'Little
Dog Turpie barks so loudly that I can't sleep. In
the morning I shall take off his tail.'

So in the morning the little old man took off
Little Dog Turpie's tail because he barked so
much.

That night when the old man and the old

woman were in bed, out of the woods came the Hobyahs. Up, up, on their long toes, creeping, creeping, through the soft grass, waving their wild tails, came the Hobyahs. And they shouted, 'Break down the house, carry off the little old man, eat up the little old woman!' But Little Dog Turpie heard them coming and he barked and he barked and he barked, 'Wow, wow!' till they ran away.

But the little old man sat up in bed and said, 'Little Dog Turpie barks too loudly, and I can't sleep. In the morning I shall take off his legs.'

So in the morning the little old man took off Little Dog Turpie's legs, because he barked so much.

The next night, when the little old man and the little old woman were in bed, out of the woods came the Hobyahs. Up, up, on their long toes, creeping, creeping, through the soft grass, waving their wild tails, came the Hobyahs. And they shouted, 'Break down the house, carry off the little old man, eat up the little old woman!' But Little Dog Turpie heard them coming, and he barked and barked and barked, till they all ran away.

But the little old man sat up in bed and said, 'That Little Dog Turpie barks too loudly, and I can't get any sleep. In the morning I shall take off his head.'

So in the morning the little old man took off Little Dog Turpie's head.

That night, when the little old man and the little old woman were in bed, out of the woods came the Hobyahs. Up, up, on their long toes, creeping, creeping, through the soft grass, waving their wild tails, came the Hobyahs. And they shouted, 'Break down the house, carry off the little old man, eat up the little old woman!' And Little Dog Turpie felt them coming, but the little old man had taken off his head, and now he couldn't bark any more and frighten them away.

So the Hobyahs broke down the house. They didn't carry off the little old man, because he hid under the kitchen table and they couldn't find him. But they carried off the little old woman to their Hobyah house, and they put her in a bag and hung her on the door-knob.

When the little old man found the Hobyahs had carried off the little old woman, he was very sorry for what he had done. Now he knew why Little Dog Turpie had been barking every night. 'I am a silly old man,' he said. 'I shall put back Little Dog Turpie's tail and his feet and his head this very minute.' So he went out into the yard and put them all back right away.

Then Little Dog Turpie went running off on his four legs to find the little old woman. He ran and he ran till he came to the Hobyah house. The Hobyahs were not at home, but they had left the little old woman hanging in the bag on the door-knob. Little Dog Turpie bit the bag with his sharp teeth till it fell off the door-knob, and then he pulled it open so that the little old woman could get out. She ran all the way back home to the little old man, and they were very pleased to see each other again, I can tell you, and they had a bit of a kiss and a hug.

But Little Dog Turpie crept inside the bag himself, and lay there waiting for the Hobyahs to come home again. Presently they came, and the

first thing they did was to poke the bag with their long fingers, for they thought it was the old woman, you see. And out jumped Little Dog Turpie, barking as loudly as he could. The Hobyahs got such a fright they all ran away, and they ran so far they never came back. And that's why there are no Hobyahs today, not one.

The man who knew better

Now this is the tale of a man who nagged.
And this is the way I tell it

Once upon a time there was a man who thought
his wife did nothing right in the house. He thought
she did *this* wrong, and *that* wrong, and that *this*
could be different, and *that* could be better. So at
last, one evening, when he came in from work, and
began grumbling and shouting the same as usual,
she said, 'Don't always be cross, my dear. We'll
change our work, you and I. You shall do my work,
and I'll do yours. Then you can show me how it
ought to be.'

The man thought it was a fine idea. So the next
morning, the woman went to work in the fields
with a scythe over her shoulder. And the man
stayed at home to keep house.

Well, he just lay about for a time, just did
nothing but scratch himself and snooze a bit and
talk to the flies crawling up the wall. He thought
it was an easy job keeping house.

Then, as time was getting on, he decided he'd

have to get a bit busy if dinner was to be ready. So he thought he'd churn the butter first. They'd need butter for dinner.

But when he'd churned for a few minutes, he felt thirsty, and thought he'd go down to the cellar for a mug of ale. Well, he went down to the cellar, and he'd just set the tap running down there, when he heard the pig come snuffling into the kitchen over his head, for he'd left all the doors open, you see. So he left the tap running with ale and dashed up the cellar steps, thinking the pig would be sure to upset the churn.

When he got into the kitchen, the pig *had* upset the churn, and was standing grunting and snuffling in among the pools of cream, making slippery cream pats wherever he moved his hooves. And of course the man slipped and slithered on those cream pats, and got more and more angry, and yelled and shouted, and managed to give the pig a terrific kick which landed it flat on the floor.

Then he suddenly remembered the tap. He dashed down the steps again, two at a time, but when he got into the cellar, every drop of ale had run out of the barrel, through the tap, and all over the cellar floor.

'Well, that's the end of that,' he said, giving the empty barrel a kick. 'I'll fill the churn with cream again, and have another go at making the butter.'

But he'd no sooner started to make the butter again when he remembered he hadn't let the cow out of the byre. She'd been shut up there since yesterday and hadn't had a bite to eat or a drop to drink all morning. So he rushed round to the byre to let her out.

He was just going to take her to the meadow – for that was her usual place, the meadow – when he suddenly remembered how late it was getting.

'It's nearly dinner-time,' he said to himself. 'I haven't time to take her up there. She'll have to go up on the roof and make the best of it.' For in the country where he lived, you see, the roofs were all thatched, and there was grass growing there. But how could he get her up on the roof, that was the question? Well, luckily the house was built against a bit of a hill, and he reckoned that if he could get hold of a plank, he could lay it from the hill up to the roof, and get the cow to walk along it.

He thought he knew where there was a plank that would do nicely. But he couldn't leave the churn in the kitchen, because the baby was crawling all over the floor and was bound to upset it; she never left anything alone, that one. The only thing he could think of to do about this, was to pick up the churn, all full of cream, and put it on his back, and he staggered out like this.

Then he suddenly thought the cow still hadn't had a drink. She certainly wouldn't find anything to drink up on the roof, so he'd better give her a drink before he got her up there. He bent down to get some water out of the well, but when he did, the churn on his back tilted and all the cream ran into his neck and his ears and his hair and dripped down into the well.

Well, after that he was feeling a bit tired, although he hadn't got very much done. But he managed to get the cow up on the roof. Now it was nearly dinner-time and he hadn't got anything ready. He decided he'd leave everything and just make some porridge. He filled the pot with water and put it on the fire. But then he suddenly thought, 'Suppose the cow falls off the roof while I'm in the kitchen.' So he hunted for a rope, and rushed outside, and climbed as fast as he could to the roof. The cow was still there.

First he tied the rope round her neck. But she didn't like it, so he tied it round her leg. Then he wondered where to tie the other end. At last he had a really clever idea. He dropped the rope down the chimney, climbed down from the roof again, nipped into the kitchen, picked up the end of the rope that had come down the chimney and tied it round his leg.

By now, the water in the porridge pot was boiling away, but he hadn't got any porridge meal ready, and it was nearly dinner-time. He ran to get the porridge meal, and just then the cow *did* fall off the roof. She only fell half-way because the rope stopped her. There she stayed, swinging in the air half-way down the wall. And the rope pulled the man by his leg half-way up the chimney, and there he stuck. Now it was dinner-time.

All this while the woman had been working hard in the field, thinking how nice it would be to come home to a dinner that someone else had cooked for her – everything ready on the table, steaming hot, and something cool and refreshing to drink. What a change that would be! But the time seemed to be a long while coming. The day went on, the sun crossed the sky, and still her husband hadn't called her. She got tired of waiting, and decided to go home.

When she got near the house she saw the poor old cow hanging half-way down the wall. 'Lawks a mercy!' she cried. She ran to the cow as fast as she could with her big scythe bumping and jabbing into her shoulder, and she took her scythe and cut through the rope, and down came the cow the rest of the way. But when she did this, the rope raced back through the chimney, and the man at the other end of it came down with a crumpled crash. The woman, of course, knew nothing about this. Only when she came into the kitchen, dearly hoping her dinner was ready, there he was standing on his head in the porridge pot.

Anansi and the pudding tree

*Now this is the tale of puddings
that grow on trees.
And this is the way I tell it*

Now Anansi was a spider. He had a friend
called Mouse. And they both had someone who
wasn't a friend at all. That was Kisander the cat.

Anansi and Mouse were frightened of Kisander.
Kisander had sharp claws and sharp teeth. And
she could pounce very quickly. She could see in the
dark when you didn't know she was there. And
she made the most horrible waily-waily noise when
she felt fierce and waved her tail in a frightening
way.

But Kisander had a dokanoo tree, a pudding
tree. And although Anansi and Mouse didn't like
Kisander, they *did* like puddings, puddings that
grew on trees. Whenever they went past Kisander's
house, Anansi would say to Mouse, 'I would love
one of these puddings from Kisander's tree.' And
Mouse would say, 'So would I.'

Kisander looked after her tree very carefully.

She dug all round it so that air would get in. She cleared all the weeds away. And she watered it all round. The puddings grew very big and round and sweet. And the bigger and rounder and sweeter they grew, the more Anansi and Mouse wanted them.

At last one night Anansi whispered to Mouse, 'Let's go to Kisander's garden and take some puddings. I'll climb up the tree and cut off the puddings with my sharp knife, and you'll stay at the bottom and tell me if Kisander is coming.'

So they crept softly in the dark into Kisander's garden, and Mouse stayed at the bottom of the tree listening, while Anansi climbed to the top. He took out his knife and cut off a pudding. It fell to the ground – 'Plop!'

When Mouse and Anansi heard that 'Plop!' they were very frightened. What a loud noise it made! It woke Kisander up in her bed in the little house, and she said out loud, 'What's happening in my garden? What's happening to my puddings? The wind must be blowing them down.' Then she turned over and went to sleep again.

Anansi and Mouse waited a moment, and then Anansi cut another pudding. It fell to the ground. 'Plop!' it said. It sounded even louder than before, and Mouse and Anansi were very frightened again.

Kisander woke up and said, 'What's happening in my garden? What's happening to my puddings? They're falling off the tree all by themselves. They must be too ripe.' Then she turned over and went to sleep again.

Mouse and Anansi waited a moment. Then Anansi took out his knife and cut another pudding. It fell to the ground. 'Plop!' it said. This time it was even louder than both the other plops because it was a very big and heavy pudding indeed; and Mouse and Anansi were very frightened. It was such a loud plop that Kisander got right out of bed and said, 'I shall see what is happening to my puddings.'

Out came Kisander into the garden. Mouse saw her two eyes shining in the dark. 'Oh dear,' said Mouse, 'I must tell Anansi.' But he didn't want to call out 'Anansi! Anansi!' because then Kisander would know who it was who was stealing her puddings. So instead he called out, 'Ceiling Thomas! Ceiling Thomas!' He thought of 'Ceiling Thomas' because Anansi was a spider and often walked on the ceiling. And then in a flash off went Mouse on his trickly little feet, and Kisander never saw him.

Kisander looked this way and that, but all she could see were three puddings lying on the ground. Anansi was curled up in a ball, quiet as quiet in the leaves of the pudding tree.

Kisander looked at the three puddings. She walked all round them one way. Then she walked all round them the other way. And she waved her tail and went waily-waily in a fierce voice.

'Someone has been cutting those puddings,' she said.

But she couldn't see anyone at all. So she picked up the puddings and went back to the house. As soon as she was gone, Anansi jumped down from the tree. 'Plop!'

'There's another pudding gone!' shouted Kisander, and she dashed out of the house again. But there wasn't any pudding on the grass. Nothing to see at all. Anansi had scuttled away as fast as he could, and he was nearly home.

'What a strange thing,' said Kisander. 'A plop, but no pudding.' So she went back to bed again, and every now and then she woke up and said, 'A plop, but no pudding.' And she never found out what had made the last plop of all.

The gingerbread man

*Now this is the tale of an old woman
and an old man who had
no children of their own.
And this is the way I tell it*

Once upon a time there was a little old woman
and a little old man. They lived together in a little
old house. They didn't have any little girls or
boys of their own, and this made them very sad. So
one day the little old woman said, 'I'll make a little
boy out of gingerbread. I'll make the dough, and
I'll roll it out, and I'll cut it into shape, then I'll
pop it in the oven to bake. And when it's done,
we'll have a little boy of our own.'

That's what she did. She made the dough, she
rolled it out, she cut it into shape, then she popped
it in the oven to bake. And when it was time for
the gingerbread boy to be done, she opened the
oven door.

Out jumped the little gingerbread boy. He
jumped out of the oven, he ran out of the kitchen,
he ran right down the street. And as he ran he
shouted,

'Run, run, as fast as you can,
You can't catch me, I'm the gingerbread man.'

And the little old man and the little old woman ran after him, but they couldn't catch him.

Then the little gingerbread boy ran on and on till he came to a cow in the meadow. When the cow saw the little gingerbread boy, she said, 'Moo, moo. Stop, stop, little gingerbread boy, you look very good to eat.' But the little gingerbread boy only laughed and ran faster than ever, and as he ran he shouted,

'I have run away from a little old woman, and a
    little old man,
And I can run away from you, I can.
Run, run, as fast as you can,
You can't catch me, I'm the gingerbread man.'

And the cow ran too, but she couldn't catch him.

Then the little gingerbread boy ran on and on till he came to a horse by the wayside. When the horse saw the little gingerbread boy, he said, 'Neigh, neigh. Stop, stop, little gingerbread boy, you look very good to eat.' But the little gingerbread boy only laughed, and ran faster than ever. And as he ran he shouted,

'I have run away from a little old woman, and a
    little old man and a cow,
And I can run away from you, I can.
Run, run, as fast as you can,
You can't catch me, I'm the gingerbread man.'

And the horse ran too, but he couldn't catch him.

Then the little gingerbread boy ran on and on till he came to some men mending the road. When the men saw the little gingerbread boy, they shouted, 'Hey, hey. Stop, stop, little gingerbread boy, you look very good to eat.' But the little gingerbread boy only laughed, and ran faster than ever, and as he ran he shouted,

'I have run away from a little old woman, and a
    little old man and a cow and a horse,
And I can run away from you, I can.
Run, run, as fast as you can,
You can't catch me, I'm the gingerbread man.'

And the men ran too, but they couldn't catch him.

Then the little gingerbread boy ran on and on and on till he came to a river. Then he stopped, because he didn't know how to cross.

While he was sitting there, wondering, a fox came along. The fox wanted to eat up the little gingerbread boy, but he didn't say so. He said, 'Do you want to cross the river?'

'Yes, I do,' said the little gingerbread boy.

'Then jump on my back,' said the fox, 'and I'll take you across.'

So the little gingerbread boy jumped on the fox's back, and the fox started to swim across the river.

When he was half-way across the fox said, 'You're not very comfortable on my back, little gingerbread boy. Jump on my neck.'

So the little gingerbread boy jumped on the

fox's neck, and the fox swam over a bit more.

Then the fox said, 'You're not very comfortable on my neck, little gingerbread boy. Jump on my head.'

So the little gingerbread boy jumped on the fox's head, and the fox swam a wee bit more.

Then the fox said, 'You're not very comfortable

on my head, little gingerbread boy. Jump on my nose.'

So the little gingerbread boy jumped on the tip of the fox's nose.

Then the fox just threw back his head, like this, and went 'Snap!', like this. And the little gingerbread boy was half gone. Then the fox did it again – Snap! – and the little gingerbread boy was three-quarters gone. Then the fox did it again –

Snap! – and the little gingerbread boy was all gone. And that was the end of the little gingerbread boy biscuit that the old woman baked that morning.

Higgledy-piggledy
and topsy-turvy

Now this is the tale of too many helpers.
And this is the way I tell it

Once upon a time there was a very busy woman.
She was busy all day long because she had so much
to do. She had the beds to make, and the floors to
scrub, and jerseys to knit, and the sheets to mend
on the sewing-machine, and the clothes to iron –
oh, and ever so many things more. And one day
she felt just plain tired of working, and she said
out loud, 'I can't manage any longer by myself. I
wish I had someone to help me.'

No sooner had she said this than there was a
knock at the front door. She opened it and there
was a little old woman. And the little old woman
said,

'Ask me in,
 Ask me inner,
 I'll help you
 If you give me dinner.'

Of course the woman was very pleased indeed, and
she asked the little old lady in. And the little old

lady began to do the ironing, while the woman got her some dinner ready.

She had just put the meat in the pan to cook when there was another knock at the door. She opened it and there was another little old woman. And this little old woman said,

'Ask me in,
Ask me inner,
I'll help you
If you give me dinner.'

So then the woman was even more pleased, and she asked the little old woman in. The little old woman began to scrub the floor, while she put some more carrots with the meat to make more dinner.

She had scarcely done this when there was another knock at the door, and there was another little old woman. And she said, just like the other two,

'Ask me in,
Ask me inner,
I'll help you
If you give me dinner.'

The woman was beginning to get a bit bothered by now, but she asked her in the same as the others, and put more onions with the meat to make more dinner. And the little old woman began to mend the sheets on the sewing-machine.

The woman had scarcely put the onions in when there was another knock at the door. And so it went on, more and more little old ladies coming to the door, and every one saying,

'Ask me in,
Ask me inner,
I'll help you
If you give me dinner.'

And now they didn't even wait to be asked to come in. They came in themselves, and they started work, one making the beds, one knitting jerseys, one doing one thing, one doing another, and eating, eating, all the time. All the time they were working they were eating, and the more the woman cooked for them and the more she baked for them, the hungrier they seemed to get. And at last she was so hot and bothered that she didn't know what to do.

So she went to her husband who was asleep in bed all this time, the lucky man, and she tried to wake him up to come and help her. She shook him and she shouted in his ear, but it was no use, he just wouldn't wake up. So she put on her hat and coat, and she went to see a wise woman who lived over the hill, and left all the little old women eating and working away, with some more bread baking in the oven.

She told the wise woman all about it, and asked her what she should do. 'First of all,' said the wise woman, 'don't ever say again you can't manage by yourself. And secondly, just go home now and when you get to your doorstep, stand there and shout "The hill's on fire!" Then all the little old women will come dashing out to have a look, and you must shut the door quickly, and as fast as you can, make everything higgledy-piggledy,

topsy-turvy, upside-down and inside out and as tingle-tangled as can be. And last of all wake up your husband by splashing some water on his face.'

So the woman thanked her and hurried away. As soon as she got to her own doorstep, she stood there and shouted out 'The hill's on fire!' And all the little old women came running out to see. And the woman quickly shut the door and started to make everything in the house higgledy-piggledy, topsy-turvy, upside-down and inside out and as tingle-tangled as could be. She turned the sewing-machine upside-down, she put the pillow at the bottom of the bed instead of at the top, she took the handle off the top of the bucket and fastened it to the bottom, she turned the clothes that were being ironed all inside out, she took the needles out of the knitting and stuck them somewhere else, and tangled the wool into knots just as if a kitten had been playing with it.

Then all the little old women outside the door began to bang and shout, 'Let us in, let us in!'

'I can't,' said the woman. 'I'm busy. I'm baking bread.'

'Bucket, come and open the door!' they shouted.

'I can't,' said the bucket. 'My handle's on the wrong end. I'm all upside-down.'

'Sewing-machine, open the door!' they shouted.

'I can't,' said the sewing-machine. 'I'm the wrong way up. I'm all topsy-turvy.'

'Bed, come and open the door!' they shouted.

'I can't,' said the bed. 'My pillow's at the bottom end. I'm all higgledy-piggledy.'

'Clothes, come and open the door,' they shouted.

'We can't,' said the clothes. 'We're all inside out.'

'Knitting, open the door!' they shouted.

'I can't. My needles are stuck in the wrong place and I'm all tingle-tangled.'

Then the little old women remembered the

bread that was baking in the oven.

'Bread, come and open the door,' they shouted.

And the bread got out of the oven and was just going to open the door for them, when the woman grabbed the bread knife and quickly cut it into slices.

Then she remembered what to do about the water. She took a cupful from the tap, and threw it over her husband who was still snoring away. He woke up in a flash, and he dashed to the door where the little old women were banging and shouting, and he shouted in a voice like thunder, 'Go away!' And they did!

The soup-stone

Now this is the tale of a very odd stone.
And this is the way I tell it

Once upon a time there was a man, and he was
very poor. He had no money to buy any food, and
so of course he was very hungry. Well, he was
walking along, wondering what he could do to get
some dinner, when he bent down and picked up a
stone from the roadway – yes, a big stone.

Then he knocked at someone's door. A woman
answered it.

'Good morning,' said the man.

'Good morning. What's that you have there?'

'Oh, that's my soup-stone.'

'What ever is a soup-stone?'

'It's a stone for making soup, of course.'

'A stone for making soup! I've never heard of
such a thing. Are there many of them?'

'Not many at all, I can tell you.'

'And does it really make good soup?'

'Oh, wonderful soup! I'll tell you what. If you
let me come in and lend me a pan, I'll show you.'

'Yes, of course, do come in. I'll get you a pan
right away.'

So the man came in, and the woman got him the

pan. He put the stone at the bottom, and covered it with plenty of water, and after a while it began to boil. The man stirred it, and peered at it, and began to hum a little. 'Hmm, hmm, lovely, lovely soup,' he said.

'Is it ready yet?' said the woman.

'Oh no, not yet,' said the man. 'But it's going to be gorgeous soup. I'll tell you what. Have you got such a thing as a carrot?'

'Yes, I have,' said the woman.

'Well if we put it in the soup, it'll be even better,' said the man. 'It'll bring the full flavour out.'

'All right,' said the woman. 'I'll get it.' So she got the carrot and they put it in the soup.

The man stirred it, and peered at it, and hummed a bit, and pretty soon he said, 'Tell you what. Have you got such a thing as an onion?'

'Would that make it better still?' asked the woman.

'Yes, it would,' said the man. 'It's gorgeous soup, but an onion would bring out the full flavour.'

So they put an onion in the soup.

The man stirred it round, and hummed the way he did, and sniffed it and peered at it, and pretty soon he said, 'I'll tell you what would be good now, to put in it. A chicken, and plenty of salt and pepper, of course.'

'Oh, of course,' said the woman. 'I'll get that.' So they put in a chicken, and plenty of salt and

pepper, and the man said the soup-stone soup
would be very good indeed.

After an hour or two, they took out everything
but the soup-stone, because the man said the soup
was almost ready; they just needed the stone to boil
a little longer to bring out the proper flavour.
Then, at last, the man lifted the stone out, and they

served the soup. My, it *was* good! That soup-stone
certainly made good soup!

'It's delicious!' said the woman. 'How
wonderful to have a stone that makes soup. I wish
I had one like that.'

'Well, there aren't many about, you know,' said
the man. 'You can't get them easily.'

'I don't suppose you can,' said the woman. 'But
my, oh my, I certainly wish I could have one, and
have soup like that all the time.'

'Well, I'll tell you what,' said the man. 'Because

you've been so kind to me, I'll give you mine, my very own soup-stone. Perhaps I'll be able to get hold of another.'

'Oh, would you really?' said the woman. 'It's very good of you. It will be wonderful to have a soup-stone and be for ever having soup.'

So the man gave her his stone, and they said goodbye.

And when the poor man was hungry again, do you know what he did? He just bent down again, and picked up another stone, and said it was a soup-stone, and that was the way he managed every time.

Jack and his friends

Now this is the tale of Jack
who set out to seek his fortune.
And this is the way I tell it

Once upon a time there was a boy called Jack, and one day he set out to seek his fortune.

He hadn't gone very far when he met a cat.

'Good morning, Jack,' said the cat. 'Where are you going?'

'Oh, I'm off to seek my fortune,' said Jack.

'May I come with you?'

'Yes, if you like.'

So off went Jack and the cat, jiggety-jog, jiggety-jog.

They hadn't gone very far when they met a dog.

'Oh, good morning,' said the dog. 'Where are you going?'

'We're going to seek our fortune,' said Jack.

'May I come too?'

'Yes, certainly.'

So off went Jack and the cat and the dog, jiggety-jog, jiggety-jog.

They hadn't gone very much farther when they met a cow.

'Hello, Jack,' said the cow. 'Where are you going?'

'I'm going to seek my fortune.'

'May I come with you?'

'Certainly, you may.'

So off went Jack and the cat and the dog and the cow, jiggety-jog, jiggety-jog.

They hadn't gone very far when they met a goat.

'Good morning, Jack,' said the goat. 'Where are you going?'

'I'm off to seek my fortune.'

'May I come too?'

'Yes, if you like.'

So off went Jack and the cat and the dog and the cow and the goat, jiggety-jog, jiggety-jog.

They hadn't gone much farther when they met a cock.

'Good morning,' said the cock. 'Where are you going?'

'I'm off to seek my fortune.'

'May I come with you?'

'Certainly,' said Jack.

So off went Jack and the cat and the dog and the cow and the goat and the cock, jiggety-jog, jiggety-jog.

Now they walked and they walked until it got dark, and they began to wonder where they would sleep that night. Presently they came to a house, and they peeped through the window. And do you know who was in that house? A lot of robbers counting their money!

So Jack said to his friends, 'When I say "Go!" make as much noise as you possibly can, and we'll frighten the robbers away.' So in a minute Jack said 'Go!' And the cat mewed, 'Miaow, miaow,' and the dog barked 'Woof! Woof!' And the cow mooed, 'Moooo, moooo.' And the goat bleated, 'Me-e-e, me-e-e,' and the cock crowed, 'Cock-a-doodle-doo! Cock-a-doodle-doo!' And

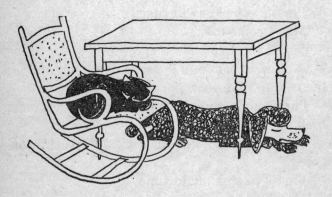

they made such a shocking noise that the robbers had a terrible fright and all ran away.

So Jack and his friends went inside the house to have a good sleep. And the cat lay down on the rocking-chair, and the dog lay under the table, and the goat lay down at the top of the stairs, and the cow went into the cellar where it was nice and cool, and the cock settled down on the roof because he liked to be up high.

In a little while it got dark, and everything

seemed to be quite quiet, and the robbers thought perhaps they could go back to their house. So they told one man to go back and see if everything was all right.

Off he went on tiptoe, stepping very quietly. But he came dashing back, all out of breath and very frightened. 'Don't send me there again!' he said. 'It's a dreadful place! I tried to sit down in the rocking-chair, but a horrible old woman stuck her knitting-needles into me.' (*That wasn't a horrible old woman. That was the cat!*) 'And I peeped under the table, and a dreadful old man got hold of me with his pincers.' (*That wasn't an old man with his pincers under the table. That was the dog!*) 'And I went up the stairs and an old woman with a sweeping-brush knocked me right down again.' (*Oh, the silly! That was the goat!*) 'Then I ran down to the cellar, but there was a man there chopping wood, and he hit me on the head with his chopper.' (*That wasn't a man with a chopper. That was the cow!*) 'But the worst one of all,' said the robber, 'was on the roof. There was a dreadful little old man up there who kept shouting, "Chuck him up to meeeee! Chuck him up to meeeee!"' (*The silly! That was the cock!*) 'I wasn't going to be chucked up to him, so I ran right out of the house! And I'll never go there again!'

So the robbers never went there again. And Jack and his friends stayed as long as they liked.

Uncle Bouki and the horse

Now this is the tale of a
trick that was played. But who was it played on?
And this is the way I tell it

One day Uncle Bouki decided to go to market.
He looked for his donkey, but he couldn't find her
anywhere, for she had run away in the night.

Now he was in a mess. 'However shall I get my
yams to market?' he said. 'I can't carry them all
myself. I shall have to go to the mean old man who
lives down the street and ask him to lend me his
horse. And he won't do *that* for nothing.'

So off he went to the house of the mean old man,
the meanest old man in the village.

'Will you lend me your horse to carry my yams
to market?' he said.

'If you give me seventy-five pence,' said the mean
old man.

'Seventy-five pence!' said Uncle Bouki. 'I've only
got fifteen!'

'Well, give me the fifteen now, and you can give
me the other sixty when you come to collect the
horse in the morning. And *see you don't load him
up too much!*'

'Well! Fifteen pence now, and the rest later! I

knew this would cost me something!' said Uncle Bouki to himself. He grumbled and grumbled, but what could he do? He had to get his yams to market somehow. So he gave the old man his fifteen pence, and that was how it was left.

Now the next morning when he got up early to call for the horse and take the yams to market, what did he see but his donkey back in the field again! She was pleased to be home, and was rolling about in the coffee plants because her back was tickly.

'Roll away!' said Uncle Bouki. 'You've got me in a jam. I shan't need the horse to go to market now, but the mean old man has taken my fifteen pence and he'll never give it back.' And he shouted at the donkey, but she just flicked her ears and rolled more happily than ever.

While he was shouting at the rolling donkey, Clever Dick came down the road. He stopped to listen to Uncle Bouki, and then he said, 'Uncle Bouki, I'll get your money back. You can rely on me.'

'That's good of you,' said Uncle Bouki.

So off they went down the road together to the house of the mean old man.

'We've come for the horse,' said Clever Dick.

'Give me the sixty pence first,' said the mean old man.

'Wait a bit,' said Clever Dick. 'First we must see if the horse is big enough'

'He's big enough,' said the mean old man. 'A horse is a horse, not an elephant.'

'Just a minute,' said Clever Dick. 'We must measure him.'

He took a tape-measure out of his pocket and began to measure the horse.

'There's eighteen inches for Uncle Bouki, in the middle,' he said. 'There's fifteen inches here for me. There's another eighteen inches for my mammy at the front. And there's twenty inches for Auntie Bouki at the back, for she's fatter even than my mammy.'

'What are you talking about!' said the mean old man. 'You can't put four people on one horse!'

'Sssh,' said Clever Dick. 'You'll muddle me. And here on the horse's neck, there's ten inches for young John. And – that's lucky! – we can just fit Boukino on John's lap, and Boukinette in his arms, without taking up one inch more.'

'You're crazy!' cried the mean old man.

'And as for the other children, they can sit between the horse's ears,' said Clever Dick, busy with his tape-measure. 'One . . . two . . . three . . . yes, they can just squeeze in if they don't mind sitting pretty tight.'

'No, no!' shouted the mean old man.

'But the trouble is,' went on Clever Dick, 'I can't see where to put the baby . . . I think we'll have to roll him up in a blanket, and tie him on to the horse's tail.'

'Tie him on to my horse's tail!' shouted the mean old man.

'Sssh,' said Clever Dick. 'That's the second time I've had to tell you. I still haven't worked everything out. Where are we going to put the pigs and goats?'

'The pigs and goats!' shouted the mean old man.

'Oh don't you worry,' said Clever Dick. 'I can see what to do. We'll put the pigs in one sack and

the goats in the other, and we'll hang them one on each side.'

'That's enough!' shouted the mean old man. 'That finishes it! Here's your fifteen pence back! You can't have my horse!'

'Fifteen pence!' said Clever Dick. 'What are you talking about? You mean seventy-five pence. You said we could have it for seventy-five pence, and now you only give us back fifteen.'

'Uncle Bouki only gave me fifteen,' said the mean old man. 'He said he'd give me the rest later.'

'Now, now,' said Clever Dick, 'you know you told him it would cost seventy-five. So seventy-five is what you have to give him back. And if you don't give it back, we'll take the horse.'

Then Uncle Bouki, looking at the horse, suddenly said, 'Good gracious! Wherever shall we put Grandma!'

'Take seventy-five pence!' shouted the mean old man. 'Take seventy-five pence and get away from my horse!' And he pushed seventy-five pence into Clever Dick's pocket, jumped on his horse and galloped away as fast as he could, not even looking behind him.

Clever Dick and Uncle Bouki began to laugh. They laughed and laughed till they held their stomachs, and tears ran down their faces, and they rolled about in the grass like the donkey in the coffee plants. When they couldn't laugh any more, they wiped their faces, and Clever Dick went down the road and Uncle Bouki went back to his house.

Back in the house Uncle Bouki began to remember it all over again. 'What a joke that was,' he said to himself. 'I gave him fifteen, and he gave me seventy-five back. *I gave him fifteen, and he gave me seventy-five back!*' He began to laugh again, and he put his hand in his pocket to feel the lovely money . . . and then a funny look came over his face. He tried another pocket. Then another. 'Clever Dick!' he roared. 'It's all in Clever Dick's pocket! He's got the seventy-five pence!'

He ran to the door and he ran down the street, but Clever Dick was nowhere to be seen. Yes, Uncle Bouki was right; what a joke that was.

So Uncle Bouki came back to the house and he sat down and closed his eyes. For a long time he made no sound at all, only a whistling noise as the breath came out of his mouth. Then suddenly he said out loud, 'I don't think we could have done it!'

'Done what?' said Auntie Bouki, who had just come into the house.

'Put Grandma on the horse,' said Uncle Bouki, and he started snoring.

The woman who always argued

*Now this is the tale of the woman
who always argued.
And this is the way I tell it*

Once upon a time, there was an old man and an old woman. The man was all right. It was the woman who was the trouble.

Whatever anyone said, she said the opposite. If the fishmonger said, 'I've some good herrings today,' she said, 'No, I want sprats.' If the butcher said, 'I've got lamb chops today,' she said, 'No, I want beef.' If anyone opened a window, she shut it. If someone shut it, she opened it. She vowed that hens were ducks, and cats were dogs, and when it was raining she said it was snowing.

As for her poor old husband, what trouble he had. He was with her all the time, you see, because they did the farming together. So you can imagine he was very tired of it.

One morning they went across the bridge to look at their cornfield.

'Ah,' said the man. 'The corn will be ready by Tuesday.'

'Monday,' said the woman.

'Very well then, Monday,' said the man. 'I'll get John and Eric to help harvest it.'

'No you won't,' said the woman. 'You'll get James and Robert.'

'All right,' said the man. 'James and Robert. We'll start at seven.'

'At six,' said his wife.

'At six,' agreed the man. 'The weather will be good for it.'

'It will be bad,' she said. 'It will pour.'

'Well, whether it rains or shines,' said the man, getting fed up, 'whether I get John or James, whether we do it Monday at seven or Tuesday at six, we'll cut it with scythes.'

'Shears,' said his wife.

'Shears?' said the man, amazed. 'Cut corn with shears? What are you talking about! We'll cut with scythes!' (For with shears, you see, you have to bend down and go snip, snip, at one tiny bit after another. But with the lovely curved scythe, you go *swoosh!* and half the corn falls down flat.) 'We'll cut with scythes!' said the man.

'Shears!' said the woman.

They went over the bridge, still arguing.

'Scythes!' said the man.

'Shears!' said the woman.

So angry was the woman that the man was arguing back, that she didn't look where she was going, and she fell off the bridge into the water.

When she bobbed up again, you'd think she'd shout 'Help!' but not her. She shouted 'Shears!' and the man only just had time to shout 'Scythes!' before she bobbed back again.

Up she came again, and 'Shears!' she shouted. The man yelled back 'Scythes!' and she disappeared again. She came up again once more, and this time there was so much water in her mouth, because she would keep opening it to argue, that she couldn't say anything at all, so as her head went back again she stuck out her hand

and with the fingers she silently went snip-snip, like shears above the water, snip-snip. Then she was gone.

'Stupid old woman!' said the man, stamping his foot. 'Stupid, obstinate, argumentative old woman!'

He went back to the village to get his friends to help him find her. They all came back to the bridge, and searched in the water. But she wasn't there.

'If the water has carried her away,' said one of them, 'she will be downstream. That is the way the river flows, and everything in the water must go with the river.'

So they went downstream and looked, but they couldn't find her.

Suddenly the old man shouted, 'What a fool I am! Everything else in the water would go with the river, it's true. But not my wife! She's bound to do the opposite. She'll be floating the other way, mark my words!'

So they ran up the stream, and sure enough, there she was, the opposite way to everything else And what do you know, she was insisting on floating right *up* the waterfall!

The man who rode
the tiger

Now this is the tale of a silly tiger,
and the man who met him.
And this is the way I tell it

Once there was a tiger, a fierce tiger. One day,
when the wind blew and the rain fell down and
there was thunder and lightning, the tiger crept
close to the wall of a little house in a village, trying
to get some shelter. If he pressed close enough, the

wind and the rain would not soak him so much; so he pressed very close and flat.

Now inside the house an old woman was shouting angrily. The roof of the little house was full of holes and the rain was coming in, soaking the furniture, and the old woman was scurrying about trying to push everything out of the way of the drips. 'Oh,' she shouted. 'This perpetual dripping! It's driving me mad!' And she gave another shout, and another wail, as more water came through. 'Oh this perpetual dripping! It's driving me mad! Two or three days of peace and quiet, that's all. Then the perpetual dripping gets me again!'

The tiger, hearing her shouts, became very frightened of the Perpetual Dripping. He had never seen a Perpetual Dripping, never even heard of one. 'It must be an enormous monster,' he thought. 'Much bigger and fiercer than a tiger. How she screams!' If it hadn't been pouring so hard, he would have run away at once, for fear the Perpetual Dripping would get him too.

As it was, he pressed close to the wall, with the storm crashing about on one side of him, and the woman's shouting on the other, wondering which he was afraid of more, the wind and the rain, or the Perpetual Dripping. And every time the woman dragged some furniture across the floor, to get it out of the way of the drips, he listened to the slithering, banging, rumbling sound, and he shook in all his four legs, and he thought, 'That is the roar of the Perpetual Dripping. I hope it doesn't get me.'

Well, while he was pressed so wretchedly against the wall, a man came along. Now the man was looking for his donkey, who had been frightened by the thunder and lightning, and had run away. In the lightning flash, he saw a large animal near the wall of the hut, and he thought it was his donkey. In lightning, you know, it is light one minute and dark the next, and you cannot see very well. He rushed up to the tiger and grabbed it by one ear, and started to scold it. 'You bad beast, you! You bad beast! Making me trudge all round in the storm! Getting me soaking wet!' And he pulled a stick from his belt and started to hit the tiger, shouting all the time.

The tiger had never been treated like this before. No one had ever grabbed him by the ear, let alone hit him. 'Goodness!' he thought. 'It's the Perpetual Dripping! It's got me too!' And he was terribly frightened.

The man pushed him and shoved him and dragged him along. The tiger didn't dare fight back, but came along as meekly as you please, because he thought it was the Perpetual Dripping. 'No wonder the old woman was frightened,' he said to himself. 'It *is* terrible.'

Then the man got on the tiger's back and made the tiger carry him home, kicking him and hitting him and shouting at him the whole time without stopping; and the tiger was very frightened. At last they reached the house, and the old man tied the tiger up to a post in front of the door and went to bed. All the rest of the night, the tiger stood shivering, thinking, 'I hope the Perpetual Dripping doesn't come back for a bit. I hope I have two or three days of peace, like the old woman said.'

Now in the morning the man's wife went out and she nearly jumped out of her skin when she saw a tiger fastened to the front door. 'Do you know what you brought home last night?' she shouted to her husband.

'Of course I do!' he shouted back. 'That wretched donkey.'

'Funny-looking donkey,' she said. 'Come and see.'

The old man grumbled because he hadn't had much sleep, but he pulled on his trousers and came to have a look. And when he saw what he had really brought home last night and had tied so firmly to the front door, he fell flat on his face and couldn't be persuaded to look again till dinner-time.

Now somehow or other – you know how one person tells another – the news spread around that this man had actually ridden on a tiger. The King came to see. When he saw that the story was true, he gave the man bags of money so that he could dress in silk and live in a beautiful house and *look* like a man who rode on a tiger. Then the King went back to his palace again, very pleased.

But one day some enemy soldiers came riding against the King. There were so many of them, that the King didn't know what to do. 'I will send for the man who rode on a tiger!' he said. 'Such a man will make mincemeat of them!' So he sent a message to the man, and together with the message he sent a huge, fierce horse for the man to come galloping to the rescue.

When the man received the message – and the horse – he was terrified. 'Now I'm in a pickle!' he said to his wife. 'I've got to help the King! I've got to drive away all the enemy soldiers! I've got to ride this horse! I've never even sat on a horse in my life, you know I haven't! And look at this one, rolling its eyes at me!'

'Don't make such a fuss,' said his wife. 'You only need practice. Just get on.'

'Just get on!' he said. 'Just get on! Would you mind telling me how I do it?'

'Jump!' said his wife.

So the man started to jump. He jumped and he jumped, but he never seemed to jump anywhere near the top of the horse.

'You'll have to jump higher,' said his wife.

'Have to jump higher!' said the man, to nobody in particular.

Still he started to jump higher, but that was no

better either. All that happened was that he fell on his nose.

'The trouble is,' said the man, 'when I jump I get muddled, because I can't remember which way to turn, and that makes me fall over.'

'The way to turn,' said his wife, 'is the way that will make your face come near the horse's face.'

'Yes, that's it,' said the man, and he jumped again, and this time he was actually on the horse's back. But his face was near the horse's tail.

'No, no!' said his wife. And he had to fall off again.

So he tried and he tried, jumping and falling, and pulling and scrabbling, and getting all tangled up with the stirrups and the reins and the horse's tail. Then just as he had decided he had had enough, he suddenly found himself sitting on the horse's back.

'Quick!' he shouted. 'Tie me on before I fall off again!'

His wife dashed up with some ropes, and quickly she tied his feet to the stirrups and then tied the stirrups under the horse, quickly she tied a rope round his waist and fastened that to the saddle, quickly she tied a rope round his shoulders and tied that to the horse's neck, quickly she tied a rope round the man's neck and tied that to the horse's tail.

By this time the horse was getting nervous,

wondering what was happening to him, and he started to run. The man shouted, 'Wife, wife! You haven't tied my hands! They're loose!'

'Fasten them into the horse's mane!' she shouted after him. And as the horse gained ground and galloped faster, the man wound the horse's mane round his hands, and held on for dear life.

They went this way and that, over fields and fences and streams and walls, kicking up the dust behind them. The wind whistled past the man's ears and his nose grew red.

'You're taking me right to those enemy soldiers!' he shouted. 'Whoa, whoa! I'm not going, I tell you!' He took one of his hands out of the horse's mane and grabbed at a little tree, thinking to stop the horse. But the horse was going so fast, and the earth that the little tree was growing in was so soft from all the rains, that the tree came up in his hand and there he was thundering along on this fierce horse, brandishing a tree in his hand.

When the enemy soldiers saw him galloping towards them like that, they were very frightened. 'Did you see!' they shouted to each other. 'He pulled up a tree to hit us with! A whole tree! This is certainly the man who rode on a tiger.' And they ran for their lives and were never seen again.

Just at that moment, the horse stopped dead, the ropes all snapped, and the man fell off the horse's back. But luckily there was no one to see.

When the man had recovered his breath, he walked home, leading the horse by the bridle. He preferred it that way, because nothing on earth, he said out loud, would ever induce him to get on a horse again. And when the people saw him coming, they said, 'What a wonderful man he is! He drove away the enemy soldiers all by himself, and instead of showing off like another man would, riding splendidly on his tiger or galloping on his fierce horse, he comes back walking on his own two legs like a perfectly ordinary person, just as if he wasn't brave at all!'

Snip
snap snover
this book's
over

Author's note

Babies are international.

Lying in his cot, babbling, a baby speaks the consonants and vowels of every race in the world. Only as he grows older does he learn the restrictions of patriotism, and in our country become English.

Learning to speak one's own language is at first a process of throwing away. A baby offers his mother one sound after another, and some she doesn't like, and some leave her indifferent, and some make her look very grave. But now and then one fills her with delight, and then the baby is filled with delight. More and more important people come running, all full of this magical delight, to hear this powerful sound, this *one*, out of the baby's vast international language, so that the baby says it again, and remembers it is well-liked.

How he has to limit himself! 'Goodbye, West Indian, Rumanian, Russian, Greek, Israeli, whom I joyfully hailed when I came innocent into the world, when my toe was in my mouth and the sky was in my grasp, when all sounds were alike to me and I didn't know I was only English. Now I am two years old and we no longer speak the same language!'

Yet though they have had to give up their international language, two-year-olds still share the same stories. All over the world the same nursery story echoes, here in one language, there in another, and the children chant the same refrain.

I have concentrated here on the gleeful ones. Small children have a wonderful sense of humour that is often beaten down by the pressure of school and society, and that needs to be fed from the start if it is to survive to appreciate human beings for what they are and can be, and to cock a snook at pretentiousness.

It has been difficult to fit a story to its original country, and sometimes I have wondered if there was any point in trying. All I have done finally is to give a suggestion – that this *may* be the country where such-and-such a tale started. At least this reminds us that our riches are not only of our making. The tales are not translations. I have retold them in English idiom so that English-speaking children will enjoy them. This is not scholarly of me, but it is deliberate. I thought it better that the tales should live with gusto, than die pedantically. I hope scholars will forgive me.

I think we do not tell stories nearly often enough to children nowadays. As soon as they can read, we punish them. 'Now that you can read for yourself,' we say, 'you needn't bother me any more.'

But children need stories to be read to them for years after they can read. There is always much more in telling a story to children of any age than just the story.

In this book I am concerned only with small ones. When a child of this age listens to a story, he is experiencing so much. He is feeling the warmth of your body, your softness and your strength. He is experiencing the wonder of how those miraculous words come out of your mouth, and, if he is very young, he will put up a hand and feel them as they come. (Only as a lover, many years later, will that child, boy or girl, trace another's face so wonderingly.) He is remembering the good things you have done together, that make you smile together when you come to certain parts of the story, parts of whose meaning is secret to you two. He is experiencing, as he does over and over again, that good things come from you to him. If we say story-telling is a gift, we mean exactly that – not that only certain people can tell stories properly, but that whoever does it for a child gives something wonderful and precious.

Tell the stories slowly, taking your time. Make the most of the words, enjoying them – 'Squoooontum,' 'Squeeeentum.' Make everything happen as you say it. 'Then he walked, and he walked, and he walked' – perhaps you sway to the left and the right and the left again, as you say it, and the children, listening, do the same. 'But mind you don't look in my bag' – and here you may shake a stern finger in time with the words, and the children, listening, frown and crinkle their brows and do the same. 'Halvor!' you cry, making the sound come, drawn-out, from a long way off through a forest of trees, and the children will listen for an echo. 'Go away!' you shout, with the magnificent, unworried power of the husband of that anxious housewife ... 'And they did,' you finish; and the children nod, matter-of-factly, meaning 'Well, naturally they would.'

The phrase that is absolutely predictable, that comes in with every story, is 'And this is the way I tell it.' It is the part every child will say with you, sure of its reliability, eagerly trusting in its ritual, settling down after it with a sigh of contentment because everything is as it should be. You must never miss this out, or think it unimportant. If you do, on just one occasion, you will have to start again and 'do it properly.' And if you have never said it at all, you have been spoiling your ship for a ha'porth of tar. For with such a secure and familiar magic sign, anything at all can happen, however wild, and still stay controlled.

I wanted George Him to illustrate this book because I knew he would do as an artist what I was trying to do as a writer. He brings his own gaiety, exuberance, and resilience. They are pictures 'for reading,' he says, not just for looking at: there are so many details to ponder on that add to the story.

Yet even so, there are sad parts in stories sometimes, and frightening parts. The same part may make one child laugh, and another cry. One child I heard of had *Little Black Sambo* read to him. All the other children in the family had loved the story so, as it came down to them; but he was found feverishly and agitatedly and tearfully wrapping the tiny book in masses of paper and yards of string to post away quickly to 'some other little boy' who could perhaps stand it better. Many children cannot bear in the Brunhoff books that Babar's mother should be killed, and Babar left alone. A child is a slightly different child each day – sometimes sad, sometimes overshadowed, sometimes asking questions you cannot hear; and a story may delight him one day, yet be too much to bear another. Then, when the personal, private fear has passed, it may delight him again. If the teller of the tales is close to the child, every fleeting expression on the child's face, every tension in the child's body, will mould the flow of the tale.

There is one story here, Little Dog Turpie, that is loved unreservedly by all the children I tell it to, except one; and when I tell it to him, I have to tell it in a warm, laughing way, that tells him that he and I are together on this, and we'll see the little old man and the little old woman and Little Dog Turpie safely through. Sometimes it helps a child like this if you join in and all

say a story together, particularly the frightening bits.
'Don't you dare come on to my bridge!' you all roar, and
feel very strong and in command of everything.
Sometimes you can both make an imperious gesture.
These ways are good, because in shouting and doing the
child can get rid of his fear, and because actually taking
part in a story that frightens him or saddens him gives
him power, and he grows a little, and also because in that
same moment he realizes it is just a story and chuckles
suddenly with delight. But sometimes you may just have
to alter the story a bit, though in this case you must write
the new words firmly into the text, otherwise a new
reader might come along before the child is ready and
read out something devastating.

Sometimes you will be telling the story to a group of
children. They will be sitting in front of you in a row,
or in several rows, their faces very grave, their eyes fixed
on you. So many faces you will have to watch for signs of
strain, so many faces you will have to speak right into,
telling your personal tale to each one child! But
sometimes all the faces will break into glee, or the
children leap to their feet and declaim with delight the
jingle that has come so many times before and makes the
story everybody's, not only the teller's.

When you know the story by heart and, as one little
girl said, 'don't tell it with the book – tell it with your
mouth', when you can speak right *into* the child, the
printed words will still be there. And sometimes, at the
child's demand, you will find you trace them with your
finger as you tell the tale; and sometimes, of course, the
child will do the telling, hopefully and flourishingly
giving a familiar word to a magic printed pattern; and so,
without ever being pressed, the child will learn to read a
little, because reading is part of shared delight, because
reading brings new friends and enchanting happenings

John Cunliffe
Giant Kippernose 45p

Sad ones, lonely ones, mischievous and nasty ones — nine stories
of nine gigantic giants : Giant Kippernose . . . who hasn't had a
bath for a hundred years, Giant Bogweed . . . just downright nasty,
Giant Mambrino . . . enemy of the Pendle witches . . .
For children aged 7 to 11.

J. W. Fortescue
The Story of a Red Deer 50p

Delightfully illustrated and full of the timeless appeal of all young
creatures, here is a book to enchant every nature-lover. From
downy-haired calf to heavy-antlered stag, the red deer, Lord of the
Forest, meets the other wild creatures who inhabit the English
countryside . . . A touch of magic for every young reader.

Ann Lawrence
The Travels of Oggy 40p

Oggy is a young, unadventurous hedgehog who lives very happily
in a garden near Hampstead Heath which belongs to 'his' family.
But when his family move to the country, Oggy gets lonely and
decides to follow them . . .

and deeper understanding into his world. And of course the pictures are still there too, always there, those wild-controlled pictures, to be chuckled over and heaved over with screwed-up shoulders and screwed-up eyes, or drunk in gravely with absorbed inwardly-radiant concentration.

I said earlier that these stories survive all over the world, and have done so for a very long time. Yet even I have poked my fingers into history, as everyone does, by the choice I have made, and by my own shifting emphasis. There are no stories here of children abandoned by their parents, nor any acceptance of the superiority of boys, or the habit of giving away girls as prizes. Folk tales have always changed, as the society that made them and received them back has changed. And every story-teller plays his part, writing or telling.

LEILA BERG